# THE CASE OF THE MISSING TRAIN

## ROBBIE & BONCHAT MYSTERY# 4

## STEVE WACHTEL

To order additional copies of this book, contact:
Xlibris
844-714-8691
www.Xlibris.com
Orders@Xlibris.com

ISBN:    Softcover        978-1-6698-3856-2
         EBook            978-1-6698-3855-5

Print information available on the last page

Rev. date: 07/18/2022

PREVIOUSLY BY STEVE WACHTEL

This Book is Dedicated to My Wife
and Life Partner, Maxine

Whoosh! Whoosh! Whoosh!
The helicopter blades sounded
Overhead, as Robbie and
Bonchat watched as the air pushed
By the churning blades rebounded
Off the stones and sand
Around them. This secluded spot
Was the rendezvous chosen
By the deep disguised voice
That had called about some vague plot
Against the President, news that froze them
In the hearing. There was no choice,

Fear was not going to hold them back
When the USA needed their help!
So, here they were, riding the bird,
Holding on, fighting a panic attack
As the copter made them yelp
Rocking and rolling in its absurd
Fashion, until finally they landed...
Camp David! Lots of Secret Service,
Giving suspicious looks as they patrolled,
The grounds. Robbie and Bonchat were handed
A thick report and searched by nervous
Hands and led through a tunnel, old
And deep underground. "Halt!" a voice resonant.

And they stood before a steel door, waiting.
Suddenly, the door swung open and they were led
Inside. They were greeted by... the President!
There he sat, at a long desk, contemplating
A single sheet of white paper. He said
Nothing at first, so they wondered at the content
On that paper. He kept reading and sighing,
Touching his hair(was that a toupee?)
And looking like he had the American continent
On his back, all problems lying
On his shoulders, a look of dismay

On his face, fingers curled in
In his hair... a look of despair.
Then he glanced up at them.
"Who brought in a cat so thin?"
He muttered. "I had a cat more fair,
The most beautiful. She was a gem!
The very finest to look upon!"
Bonchat rolled her eyes and Robbie shrugged.
"Er.. Mr. president," he interjected, Sir..."
But President Ligner went on and on..
His eyes were strange, looked drugged-
Bonchat leaped on his lap, began to purr
The President grew silent, spell gone...
President Ligner sighed, and spoke

"Now what are you two here about...
Oh, yes, something about losing...
Which is strange, really a joke,
Because there really is no doubt
I Never lose! Oh, so confusing..."
Robbie ventured. " Sir, we came
Because we were told, well, you have
Been losing your train of thought..."
"Well, that would be a shame..."
The President muttered "No salve
For that wound. Am I caught
In that trap? Fake news..."

The President's Chief of Staff
Took them to the side.
"It is not nice to confuse
President like that. Don't laugh!
We brought you here to provide
An answer to this mystery.
So, we expect you to find
His train of thought, and soon!
We are told you two have a history
Of solving riddles, to see where others are blind.
Not that the President needs a tune
Up... well, you'll know what to do..."
As they were led away,

Bonchat & Robbie agreed
It would take more than they two,
They would need their friends if they
Had any real hope to succeed,
to work this mystery through.
So, back home they went
Where they met Doby Dragon,
Wally Wizard, Peggy Peahen too!.
They set out on their quest-event,
Solving this, for years they could brag on...
find a train... but where?
Wait! Of course! At a station!
"Oh, station master, seen a train?
He laughed. "Every day, everywhere!
Only thing I do see!"but..(added in frustration)
A train of thought?never! Boggles my brain!
They thanked him and continued on their way.
Where to look next?... of course!
Wally Wizard waved his wand and
They found themselves in the subway!
So many people, rushing, tumbled and tossed...
They could barely find a place to stand!
No one stopped to answer their plea.

Let's go! Robbie said with a sigh.
These people are ruder than a politician!
Where next? They couldn't agree!
But Bonchat looked Robbie in the eye,
And, with a flip of her tail, made the decision...
She pranced off and they followed,
For she had found, as only she could,
A secret passageway. Down and down
They went, for someone had hollowed
Out an underground playhouse, good
And well hidden from Gotham town
Above. They twisted and turned,

Bonchat pointing the way
Through a stone cavern maze.
Finally, into a chamber where lights burned
And it was brighter, brighter than day.
Where they found, Walter Wizard, whose gaze
Was not happy or kind. For he disliked
Being discovered. He was Wally's brother!
But he was the very opposite in makeup.
Hated people! They were no way alike.
But what caught their eyes was another
Thing... a thing that made them all wake up
And take notice!it was a big, no, huge,
*No ginormic! Electric train set*, only of course
It needed no electricity, only Wizard's fire.
They all stared, then sought refuge
In each other, to find the resource
Within to overcome the wizards mad desire.
For this was the President's train of thought!
"begone fools!" Shouted Walter Wizard.
This is mine and it will stay mine!
You trespassed and were caught!
Leave before I turn you into a lizard!
"Don"t do this!" They whined.
"That train is not yours and besides,
It is a strange train of thought."

Walter Wizard just chuckled madly.
"I never had a train that rides
Like this one, never as it ought
To! Never a train in my youth, sadly.
I will never surrender it... never!
And with that, he raised his wand,
To strike them all with a spell.
Wally leaped up, a terrible error,
For his fire was soon gone,
And Walter, with a furious yell,
Would surely have severed
His head, if not for Bonchat's magic purr,
A purr that flowed into Wally's fire,
Intensifying it, (she was so clever!)
Binding Walter's wand, and then in a blur,
Suddenly, he was gone! And The entire
Train set with him! "I am wholly
Confused, said Robbie. What happened?"
Wally, clearly shaken, began to explain.
In a low voice and slowly...
"Walter would have baked us with a zap and

The hate from his mad flame.
It was only Bonchat bless her forever!
Who could resist the magic, because she has
Her own animal magic! So strong!
I have found in our time working together.
She saved us and I think the President as
Well! Bonchat gave the others a long
Look. A smirk in her eyes or not?
A triumph she long would feed on!
Well, they had together sought
To solve a mystery, unravel a knot
And succeeded! One thing they all agreed on:
President Ligner had the strangest train of thought!

Printed in the United States
by Baker & Taylor Publisher Services